GW00865451

Peter the Penguin
and the Iceberg from the North

Written by: **Tim Jones**
Illustrated by: **Cher Ainscough**

Peter the Penguin
and the Iceberg from the North.

by: Tim Jones
illustrations: Cher Ainscough
design: Janina Zylinska

ISBN 978-1491099384

www.peterwestropp.co.uk

for Peter

One sunny morning in Antarctica, Peter the Penguin was cooling off on his favourite icy slide while he looked out to sea to find his breakfast.

Peter loved to wear colourful clothes because they brightened up everybody's day. Whatever he wore, it was always gaudy and it always made his friends laugh.

That morning he had chosen a pink bowtie, as pink as a peach, to wear over his black and white penguin wetsuit. He'd also picked out his best orange cape, which was as bright as a starfish.

Suddenly Peter saw a shoal of fish breaking the surface of the sea in the distance. He dived down the ice-slide and into the waves with a happy splash.

Peter loved to chase fish. That morning's shoal was his favourite kind. They weren't too fast and they weren't too slow and the little penguin had to swim as quickly as his little orange feet would propel him to keep up. As he swam he dodged the huge icebergs, which drifted slowly in the sea like giant mints.

Suddenly there was a swoop from the sky, then a shadow and a great flap of wings. Peter ducked as a huge bird landed in the sea in front of him with a splash.

The little penguin blinked the salty water from his eyes.
There on a wave tucking in her enormous wings was
Alice the Albatross. The big-billed bird was one of his
greatest friends. They'd known each other since they
were eggs. Alice's little face-feathers were all a-flustered.

'Peter, Peter, you have to come and see,' Alice squawked
as she struggled to catch her breath. 'You won't believe
your eyes. Quick! Follow me!'

Alice took off with a lurch to the north and Peter dived to follow her, a little disappointed that he'd have to skip breakfast.

The pair swam and flew into the wind and waves, joking with each other through the spray.
'How's the water?' Alice called.
'Cold and blue,' replied Peter. 'How's the sky?'
'Same,' said Alice.

As the icebergs cleared, and the ocean began to calm Peter realized he had never come this far before. A mist had fallen and the air felt warm and strange. Alice circled silently above as a huge iceberg floated into view. On top of it was a creature that Peter had never seen before.

The great beast sat at the front of a family of similar animals. It had white fur and a big black nose. Its paws were enormous and its teeth and claws looked extremely sharp.

Peter stopped swimming, fearful of the strange creatures. But before he could dive deep to try and hide beneath the waves, the largest one spotted him and opened his great mouth, then roared.

'Swimming bird, we are polar bears.'

'We come from the North and seek a new home.'

Peter covered his ears in
fright. He had never heard
a voice so loud.

'Our journey has been long and our bellies are empty.
Our home has melted and we are running out of time.
We need ice to live on. Do you know these seas?'

Peter tried his hardest to be brave.

'I am Peter and I am a penguin. Where I live there is more ice than you could ever imagine. I could show you the way?'

The bears licked their lips. One of the small bears asked.

'What's a penguin, Mummy? Is it a snack, like a seal?'

'Come and ride on our iceberg and show us the way,' the big bear said and reached out his massive paw towards Peter.

Out of the blue the water around him churned and Peter was lifted out of the sea on what seemed like a slippery black island. He suddenly realised he was riding on a whale's tail. His huge friend, Hercules the Humpback, had heard the polar bear's roars and had come to the rescue. He burst from the waves below.

'Hold on,' Hercules sang. 'It's not safe. Polar bears eat little birds like you. As for the seals, you must warn them. Swim as fast as you can.'

'Oh, dear!' said Peter. 'What trouble I've caused.'

The pod of whales surged from the deep and began to push the iceberg north, back to where the bears had come from. The big bear paddled as hard as he could but the whales were too strong.

One of the baby bears burst into tears. 'We have nowhere to go. Our iceberg will melt. We just want somewhere to live,' it cried. Peter heard the little bear and felt so sad that he could not help.

Then he had an idea.

He told Alice his plan and the albatross flew to the bears to negotiate from a safe height.

Peter swam as fast as he could to the seals and broke the news about the bears. The seals took it badly. Some of them jumped straight into the sea. Others tried to waddle off inland towards the distant mountains to hide. One seal just buried his head in the snow.

'They can't come here!' said one.
'They'll eat us all!' said another.

'Stop. Stop,' quacked Peter. 'I have an idea. We can all live together. Please. Listen to my plan.'

Peter told the seals his idea and after much seal-barking and flipper-flapping they nervously agreed.

The little penguin headed straight to his secret snow cave where he kept all of his colourful clothes.

Soon Alice arrived with her albatross friends and began to carry the bright costumes off through the air.

As they flew, the neon clothing in their bills looked like brilliant kites in the southern sky.

Later the seals watched as Hercules and the other whales escorted the iceberg towards their new home. But before the visitors were allowed to put one paw on the ice, Peter made them all agree some rules.

No snacking on seals.
No snacking on penguins.
No scaring little ones.
And finally...

Neon clothing at all times!

The seals were safe and the penguins were happy and the polar bears had somewhere new and cold to live. The seals upheld their end of the deal and fished for the polar bears as well as themselves. Peter threw a big party to celebrate.

Even in the thickest snow, the polar bears could always be seen. So as the sun set on that wonderful day, Antarctica was at peace and Peter content. He had more friends and more colourful clothing.

Peter the Penguin couldn't have been happier.

The Peter Westropp Memorial Trust supports the many carers who provide unpaid assistance to those unable to cope on their own. The trust supports the contribution made by this largely unrecognised group for three main reasons.

Firstly, if Peter had survived it's likely that he would have required significant support from those around him.

Secondly, most of us will at some stage in our lives be relied upon to support others; unwell or handicapped children, aging relatives or ill or injured friends.

Thirdly, a big part of Peter's life was his empathy with other people. Whether he was with family, friends, or making a first introduction, he was someone who appreciated and really connected with those around him; he genuinely was someone who really cared.

www.peterwestropp.co.uk

5023702R10015

Printed in Great Britain
by Amazon.co.uk, Ltd.,
Marston Gate.